E   Winter, Klaus   C.1

la

DATE			

Klaus Winter

Helmut Bischoff

Hoppla – Hoppla
FARMERMAN

CHILDRENS PRESS, INC.

It is night. It is quiet as a shadow
on the farm. The barn is closed. The moon
is high. The house is dark. Sh! People sleep.

The farmer sleeps. His wife sleeps. Even the cat sleeps.
Then suddenly the alarm clock rings. BRRRrrrrrrring!
Wake up! Wake up! The busy day begins.

The rooster crows. Wake up! Wake up!

The warm sun rises. It is brighter than
the light in the farmer's window.

The hens wake up. They hear the farmer's wife
who comes to feed them. Birds come, too, to eat
the scattered grain.

Hoppla, hoppla. Hop to it! There is work to do
on a little farm. Tom brings the bread. Mother
brings the milk. Tina goes to call her father.
Everyone is busy but the cat that sits and curls
his tail around his feet.

Tom goes off to watch the geese. Tina goes to tend the goats.

Father goes to load the wagon. Grandma goes for herbs and berries.

Mother stays home and works in the house all day.
   Tom's geese are bad ones. They stretch their necks
and hiss at him. They nip his heels. They flap their
wings and honk at him. The old gander runs away.

The gander stops to scold a frog.

The frog thinks, "You come any closer, you old goose,
and I will jump on your head."

Tina's goats jump around and butt each other.
They try to eat her flowers.
"Oh, how I wish I had nice, quiet geese to
take care of, instead of goats," thinks Tina.

A shepherd comes by with his big
ram and his quiet, woolly sheep.
He has a dog to help him.

The farmer comes to get his big bull. The bull can help the horse pull the heavy wagon. The old, lazy pig just grunts, and rolls over in the pen.

The horse and the bull are ready.

They will pull the heavy wagon to market.

Grandma is busy in the deep woods.
Her sharp eyes help her find many
herbs and berries.

The work is almost done. The day is almost gone.
The farmer is tired and hungry. But he cannot eat
and rest until his animals are fed and in the barn.

How good the supper smells! There are herbs in the
noodles and berries in the pie.

Everyone is glad that the day's work is done. Soon
they will sleep. Only the lazy cat stays awake. He has
slept all day, so he sits on the roof and howls at the moon.